For Maureen and John

First published 2011 by Macmillan Children's Books. This edition published 2012 by
Macmillan Children's Books, a division of Macmillan Publishers Limited, 20 New Wharf Road,
London N1 9RR. Basingstoke and Oxford. Associated companies throughout the world.

ISBN: 978-0-330-52221-2
Copyright © Emily Gravett 2011. Moral rights asserted. All rights reserved.
10 9 8 7 6 5 4 3 2 1
A CIP catalogue record for this book is available from the British Library.

www.panmacmillan.com
www.emilygravett.com
Printed in China

THE THREE PIGS PROUDLY PRESENT

WOLF WON'T BITE!

FROM EMILY GRAVETT &
MACMILLAN CHILDREN'S BOOKS

ROLL UP!

ROLL UP!

ROLL UP!

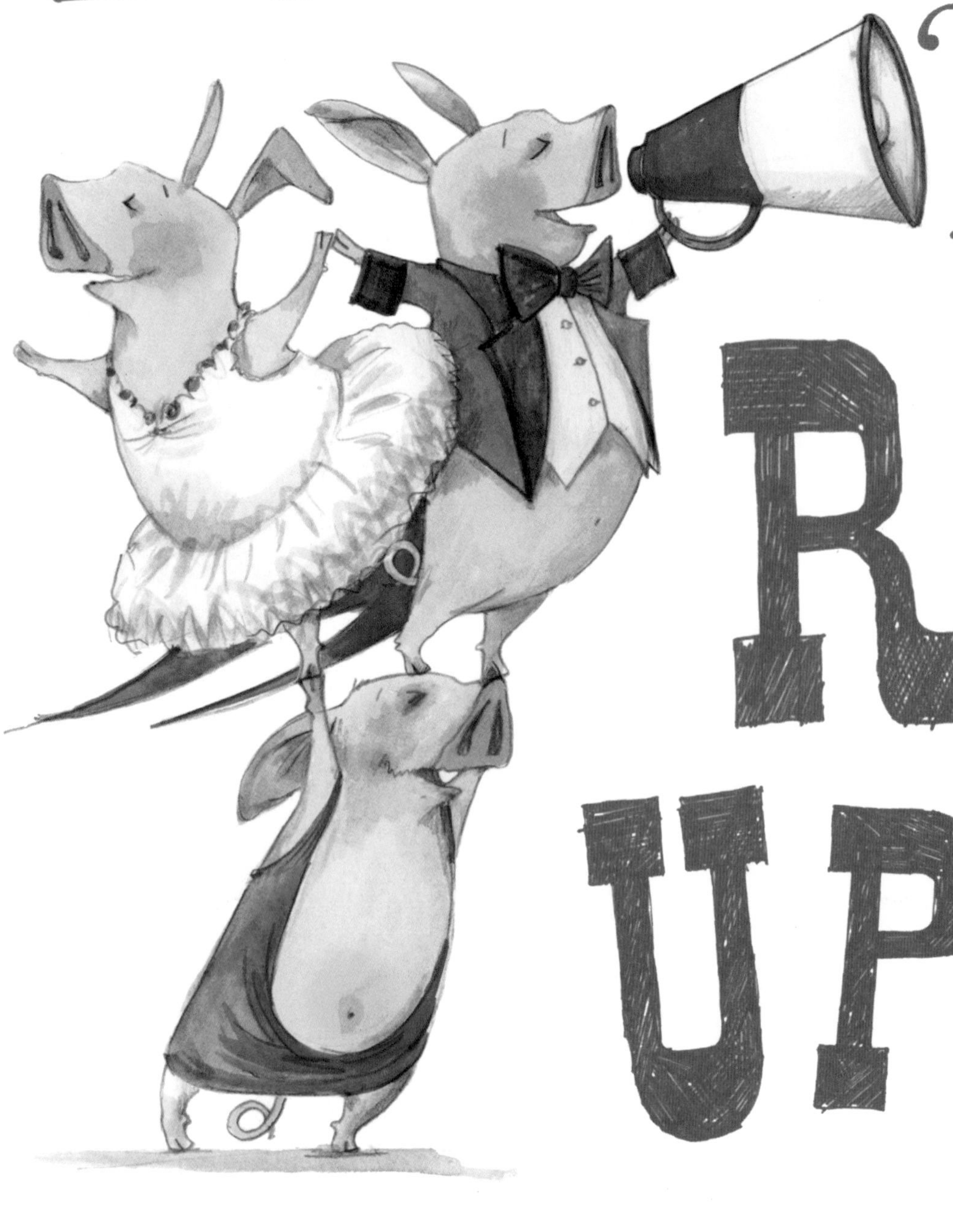

We have caught a **WILD WOLF!**

I can stand him on a stool!

I can dress him in a bow...

I can ride him like a horse but WOLF WON'T BITE!

I can make him jump

through hoops!

I can lift him off the ground !

I can make
him dance
a jig but…

WOLF WON'T BITE!

I can miss him EVERY time!

I can shoot him

through the air!

I can saw him into two, but...

WOLF WON'T BITE!

We can even
place our heads

between his

mighty
jaws

but
WOLF
WON'T...

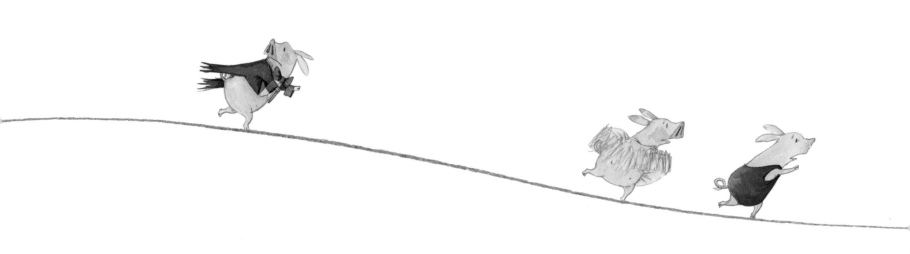